Step Into the Night

by Joanne Ryder

illustrated by Dennis Nolan

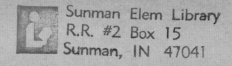
Four Winds Press

New York

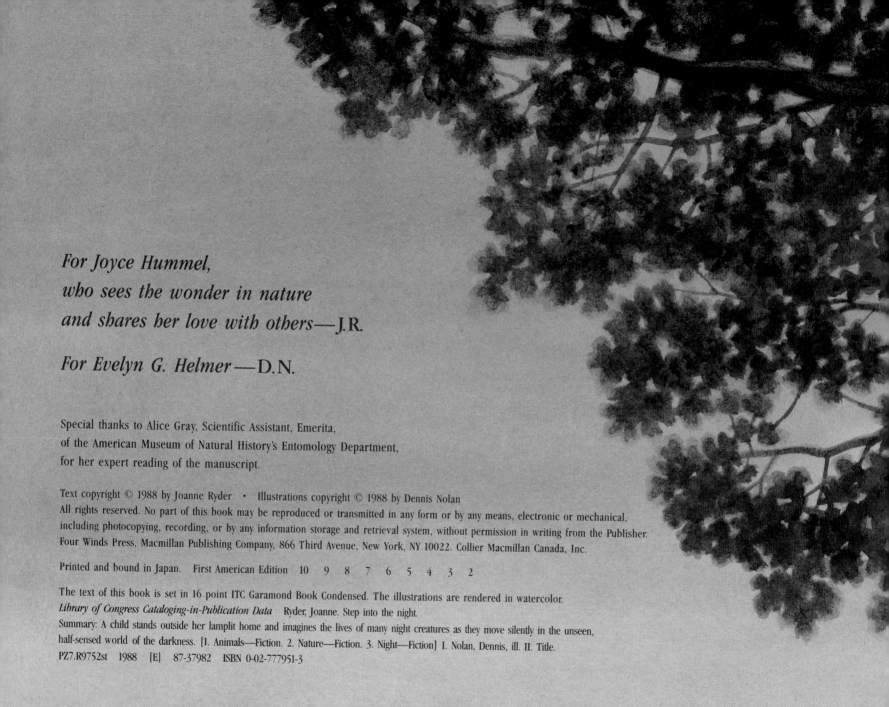

For Joyce Hummel,
who sees the wonder in nature
and shares her love with others—J.R.

For Evelyn G. Helmer—D.N.

Special thanks to Alice Gray, Scientific Assistant, Emerita,
of the American Museum of Natural History's Entomology Department,
for her expert reading of the manuscript.

Printed and bound in Japan.   First American Edition   10   9   8   7   6   5   4   3   2

The text of this book is set in 16 point ITC Garamond Book Condensed. The illustrations are rendered in watercolor.
Library of Congress Cataloging-in-Publication Data   Ryder, Joanne. Step into the night.
Summary: A child stands outside her lamplit home and imagines the lives of many night creatures as they move silently in the unseen,
half-sensed world of the darkness. [1. Animals—Fiction. 2. Nature—Fiction. 3. Night—Fiction] I. Nolan, Dennis, ill. II. Title.
PZ7.R9752st 1988   [E]   87-37982   ISBN 0-02-777951-3

When the sun hides
behind the dark rooftops,
you can step outside
and see the night begin.

All around you, grayness is creeping,
darkening the wood fence,
darkening the green bushes,
darkening the tall roosting tree.

Listen to the sparrows
chirping to each other,
chirping good night.
Fluffed up fat, the sparrows
hold tightly to the branches,
shut their eyes, and sleep.

All around you, others are hiding.
Behind small leafy curtains
tired ones rest after the long warm day.
You find a good place to rest too.

You are a shadow
against the tall dark tree.
You lean back and rest
as quiet and still as you can.
You try to be part of the tree,
waiting till the night ones stir.

Near your legs, vines tangle
into a carpet of leaves.
Something makes the leafy carpet
move and twitch and sigh—
someone small,
someone eager,
someone looking for food
and finding it.

You are a month old—
old enough to leave the old bird's nest
your mother chose to make your home,
old enough to find your way alone,
a small explorer in a new world.

Under the vines you creep,
your nose twitching,
leading you to something wonderful—
soft berries, eat-me red.
Hmmmm! Taste them!
The first berries
seem always the sweetest, the best.

A chunk of moon
shines above the treetops.
One tiny light
peeks through the evening sky
and flickers brightly far, far away.
Much closer—
but just out of reach—
another light flashes and dims.
A small flyer drifts into the bushes,
taking his flashing light with him.

Dark in the darkness, you glide slowly,
beating your thin long wings.
You dip down over the bushes and rise,
and the tip of your long body glows yellow,
darkens, then shines again.
You are a signal maker,
sending messages in the dark
to someone like you hiding below.
Will she see your tiny light?
Will she answer?

A small ball of light flashes!
You follow her light,
gliding down and down,
landing on your six legs,
crawling along twigs, over leaves
toward the light, toward the firefly
flashing so you can meet.

Behind the dark fence
yellow buds uncurl and open.
You cannot see the flowers,
but you smell them—lemony and sweet.
Ooooh! You wrinkle up your nose
as the wind carries
another scent from the woods.
It is strong and musky,
a fighting scent of someone
angry or afraid or ...

You flip over the old log, soft and rotten.
Small ones wiggle down the bark into the ground.
You hunt and dig them up, catching each one.
You are hungry and they taste good.

Crusssh russhh pit pit pit,
Someone runs toward you and you turn.
You stamp your feet and lift your tail in warning.
But the runner does not stop,
too young to have ever seen a skunk before.
You defend yourself without touching him.
He yells and squeals and runs off into the blackness.
Your scent clings to him, teaching him something new—
Let the striped one have the right of way.
Let it walk where it wishes. Let it be alone.

Clouds capture the chunk of moon,
but it escapes for a moment.
The moonlight reveals
a patch of lace
across an empty space.
You move closer
and watch a fat body
with so many legs
climbing in circles
around and around
a pale silken web.
Then the clouds find the moon,
and it and the web
disappear.

You walk high above the ground
on fine, tight lines of silk.
You stretch a new line
behind you, tucking it in place
on your wide round web.
This is a good spot for a trap.
Today, a few tiny flyers
landed by surprise
on your sticky web, tangling it.
You ate them all
and pulled your tangled web apart
and ate it too.
Tonight, you make a new one;
then you wait.
Spider time is slow
waiting for meals
to fly to you.

Overhead, you see something flutter,
blotting out stars as it passes above you.
With a high voice it calls out
more softly than the sparrows.
An old man walking by waves at you
but cannot hear the sound.
Yet the dog by his side looks up.
You and the dog listen
as the thin chirps fade away.

You look like a mouse with wide wings.
As you fly, you call and listen
to the echoes of your cries
bouncing off twigs and leaves,
bouncing back to you.
You hear an echo
bouncing off someone fluttering nearby.
A moth dances in the air
up and down, here and there,
but you trace her path
until you catch her.
As you hunt,
a young bat rests
clinging to your soft furry chest,
listening as you chirp your way
through the dark.

Even though you try to be,
you are not a tree!
You need to move and stretch
and wiggle your stiff fingers.
When you lean back,
the ground under your hand
seems to shift for a moment,
taking a new shape
as if something moved
the earth
between it and you.
Did it?

You feel something
thump above you
and dig away quickly,
swimming through the soil,
diving deeper
into the safe earth.
Your broad strong paws
scoop earth and push you
forward, away from danger,
toward places where small worms
curl and the dark firm earth
holds you safely, quietly
all around.

The night is full of voices.
You hear the cries and wonder,
Who is calling?
What are they saying?
But then you hear someone
calling over and over
till others join in,
each seeming to say,
I am here. Can you hear me?

In the dark cool water,
you kick and kick
your fat green legs
and glide to a good place.
Others splash nearby,
finding places of their own.
You are one singer
floating in the darkness.
Your throat swells with air
and you call over and over
in your deep rough voice.
Jug a rum! Jug a rum! Jug a rum!

Listen.
Someone is calling your name,
calling you back from the night.
Now the moon follows you
up the path to your door,
and you leave the night behind,
blinking as you step into brightness.
Good night! Good night, everyone!